Black Dog, Grey Lady

A Raven at Random Novella

Maggie Secara

Los Angeles

Popinjay Press

Copyright © 2017 by Maggie Secara

ISBN 978-0-9818401-4-7

Please visit Maggie's website at http://www.maggiesecara.com.

Chat with Maggie and the gang on Facebook at
https://www.facebook.com/groups/maggiesworlds/

for Kier

Black Dog, Grey Lady

i

After the dreadful business in Persia, I am sure no one will be surprised to learn that I have abandoned my studies of the mystic East in favor of our native magical lore. I have also concluded that even English magic is best explored not at the so-called witching hour but in the pleasant light of day with the library windows flung open to the air. This was proved a few weeks ago, when I looked up shivering from my work, and was relieved to find only a heavy mist from the river lurking at the windows—an honest English fog, and nothing more. Nothing with teeth.

Still, damp air is threat enough to old books, so I hurried to close and latch the casements myself rather than ring for a maid. Thus it was that as I returned to opening many a quaint and curious volume of forgotten lore, as the poet says, I discovered a note folded around a long sable feather.

"Come to the choir at once," it read, "where late the sweet birds sang."

There was no signature, but the familiar, hasty hand was dear to me, and so at once I had Polly pack a bag or two, including my pistol; and we set out together for the manor of Corbisend, near the pleasantly unhaunted village of Combe Beckett.

One might well ask why I should suppose that a note found by chance in a book seldom opened was meant for me and was not, like the book, simply a relic of antique scholarship. I may be no more than an amateur paraphysical observer, but I had no doubts. And when we arrived a few hours later, my instinct was quickly proved.

Random Corwyn flung back the door in rolled shirtsleeves and half-buttoned waistcoat, vibrating with excitement. His clear sapphire eyes fairly danced with delight when he saw me.

"Violet! Oh my dear girl, this is excellent! Come in, come in!"

Tall and slender, sharp-featured, stylish: Mr. Corwyn of London, San Francisco, and Corbisend is a worldly young gentleman, somewhat older than I—or so I believe. Whatever his age, he is a jumble of friendliness and reserve, astonishing hauteur and puckish mischief. In truth, I've never known quite how to describe him since we first met in my brother's rooms at Cambridge, before Peter's accident, and that was some years ago.

After hurriedly bestowing my coat, bonnet, and Polly on his grumbling but faithful butler, Random ushered me up the stairs and into the library. No, not the library you've seen but the one beyond the arched, apparently brass bound door that looks to have been made for children, or elves. Surely you've seen it and supposed, if you gave it any thought at all, that it was a sort of folly, a bit of whimsy, and in fact it is. However, this whimsical *trompe l'oeil* masks the true entrance to Mr. Corwyn's fabulous cabinet of curiosities, a room—nay, a suite—filled with wonders gathered from the ends of the earth.

I expected to be delighted; in fact I was somewhat bemused, for the main room had taken on the nature of a workshop. Gas lamps ringed the walls above work benches crowded in among the orderly collections of toadstones, mermaid skeletons, and unicorn horns. Every surface was buried in books, scrolls, or half-opened packing boxes. A bronze Assyrian fish goddess leered at me across a new microscope; the marble copy of a Roman emperor's sandaled foot did duty as a paperweight.

At least the wall of fan-topped French doors, usually curtained, had not changed: all stood open to admit across the balcony a golden moorland afternoon that would be hours in fading. Even so, a damp, slightly mildewed odor hung in the air. Someone, I thought, should look to his drains.

"Stand there," he ordered. Unaided but willing, I stepped carefully up onto the low box indicated and waited, giving some thought as is my habit to my immediate surroundings while he bustled about.

Clearly experiments had been occupying his time of late. A number of curious instruments—or as Random sometimes calls them, *toys*—sat, stood, or squatted on a long table within easy reach of my left hand.

While I surveyed the mysteries, Random shoved papers aside, lifted the marble foot to let a parchment scroll snap shut, penciled a few lines into a notebook, and ignored me. It is no good trying to correct his rather bohemian manners, but the urge to do so is powerful.

"I'm very well, thank you, Mr. Corwyn," I said reprovingly. "The journey was without incident and yes, tea would be lovely."

"What? No. Yes. Tea? Daniel!" All at once, his frenetic energy found direction. "Now put your left hand on that— No, the other one. That's it."

It was a broad metal disk set into a wooden base that might once have been a collar box. Into my other hand he placed a tapered glass rod the size of a buttonhook. "Hold this, tightly please. Thank you. Now stand quite still, and do not move."

"May I breathe?"

Finger to lips. "Pray do not speak."

Then all was still.

From somewhere in the clutter a violin, his beautiful Stradivarius, came into his hands, and he began to play. Music has always been Random's principal talent, and though he pursues many arts, his great gift is for the violin. But today, he had played no more than a few lilting measures when the room went suddenly dark, and the air was rent with the most pitiable moan. I thought at first it was simply the music but it was a terrible sound, fraught with despair out of the depths of nightmare.

Fortunately I am not easily startled, and rather than drop the glass rod, or remove my hand from the tingling metal disk, I froze, chilled by the horrible sound. I may have swayed on my feet a bit. Gradually some light returned, but not the light of a summer afternoon. Rather, it was as if all the color had drained out of the world, leaving only shadows and vague forms. The damp bitter smell I had noted earlier wrinkled my nose and, if I am honest, my stomach as well.

"Now, Violet." Random's firm voice came to me as across a distance, as if he were speaking in another room. In another country. "Tell me what you see."

"Nothing," I replied after a moment. My own voice fell flat and dull at my feet.

"No, no, no, Miss Delacourt. Your report, if you please. What do you *see*?"

The sharp words had their intended effect, and this time I answered promptly. "Shadows, *magister*. I see shadows. There is a kind of mottled mist, dark in places and pale in others. There is movement among the shadows, but there is no apparent order to it. Some lights—sparks or candle flames—are darting about here and there. I have the impression that the darker shapes, which are slower or static, are objects. Some might be human forms, but without more details, I cannot guess. They are like, like the furniture in a shut-up house, hidden under dust-covers."

"Is it a house? This house?"

"I cannot tell. I think not. Perhaps."

"And what else?"

"Cold. I am very cold."

Out of a gloom almost palpable, an agitation in the air swirled and tumbled like a building thunderstorm forming at a great distance. I thought of the portal we had encountered at Montségur, a door between worlds, and braced myself to resist its draw. It did not come. As I watched, a human hand emerged from the storm's eye followed swiftly by the pale face and form of a young girl coming toward me out of a billowing cloud. Around her the air hissed and whistled, and whipped her hair about staring eyes, blue eyes in a delicately tinted face. Color, where all else was grey and white. Ghost or lost spirit, she looked so very melancholy that I longed to reach out to her, to offer some comfort.

"Poor child!" I murmured, or so it seemed to me.

"Do not move!" cried Random.

Again that terrible moan tore at my heart until it nearly broke with hopelessness. I must have made some little sound of distress, if not enough to cause the fuss that followed, for I was aware of Random barking an order to someone, and other people gathering—in some room, somewhere. Then very clearly he hissed, "Violet! What is it? What is wrong?"

"Ah! It is the saddest thing in the world!"

At that, my breath caught, and my training fled, and though I never cry—never since Peter died—hot tears washed my cheeks as I gave in to an overwhelming grief.

"Miss?" Polly's voice floated past me, as did a few others though I couldn't name their owners and did not seek to.

"Do not touch her!"

Hollow-eyed, the phantasm closed the space between us until, without pausing, her little hand touched my shoulder with fingers of ice, and then the entirety of the spectral form passed like a sigh into my breast. One second, two seconds, passed. I felt the frigid presence within, spreading tendrils of snow along my limbs, into my throat and eyes, until I saw the moving light and shadow as through a hoar-frosted window fanned with ice. I was freezing to death, alone, and in silence but for the music, all the time aware of a curiosity and an idle cruelty, a thread of fear that bound the girl's sanity and threatened my own.

The rhythm of the music bade me breathe, and so I did, exhaling a cloud of stale, bitter air; inhaling a shudder.

A third second passed, and a fourth, before the phantasm abandoned me almost as if it were shaking me off in disgust. I gasped at its withdrawal; the glass rod slipped from my nerveless fingers.

"Violet!"

The dear man caught me as I fell, losing contact with the other of his devices, though I assured him I was in no danger. At least I thought I had communicated that point. Certainly I intended to. But the next thing I knew, Polly was wafting a vial of *sal volatile* under my nose. I had, to my utter mortification, fainted dead away.

I sat up at once, coughing on the fumes. Evidently I had been unconscious long enough to be removed to a tufted *chaise longue* at the other side of the room. Now I swung my feet to the floor, and attempted to restore the ruins of both my ensemble and my dignity.

"I may be a genteel lady novelist, Mr. Corwyn, but I am not one of those silly damsels, forever fainting and being rescued. Not in the least, as you well know."

"My dear," Random said, waving away the servants, "you are a lioness."

I had no answer to that except a curt nod of acknowledgement

"That being so, Miss Delacourt, will you proceed with the remainder of your report?"

The sharply formal address, so at contrast with his solicitude, snapped me again into the mode of a trained paraphysical observer, as it was meant to. Whilst I consumed an unladylike but restorative quantity of tea and sandwiches, I described my experience clearly and precisely, though there was little enough to say. My friend paced the room, barking questions I could not answer, until silence closed between us. My curiosity had been satisfied no more than his, and my ignorance was greater.

"Now," I said at last, dusting crumbs from my travelling suit. "I believe it is my turn."

"What?"

Random turned from the window where he stood to regard me with the strangest expression: thoughtful but remote, the sapphire eyes as hard as the stone whose color they borrowed. Almost as if he were someone else entirely, someone I had never met. Then he blinked twice, and was himself again. He shook his head, and for the first time since my arrival, it seemed, he actually looked at me.

"Yes, questions. Quite right. But I must review my notes; and you, dear heart, look at you! Come all this way on a moment's notice, subjected to a mad ghost, and quizzed... Well, I imagine you'd like to go up and change."

And so I did. Thankfully the housekeeper, the divine Mrs. Jenkins, has kept a room for me at Corbisend since Peter died and I took his place as Random's pupil; I need never want for comfort or a choice of costume when I find myself there. With Polly's help I gratefully cast off the rumpled travelling suit to wash my face and hands. She brushed, re-plaited, and pinned up my hair, and finally buttoned me into a softly pleated gown of sea-green silk in the graceful style they call 'aesthetic', *sans* stays, *sans* bustle, until I was *á la mode* for my station and taste.

All this is mentioned so that you may better picture the scene, not for any vanity of mine. You know perfectly well that I live for study and service; it is only that, as someone said, I prefer to live in beauty. Had I arrived wearing such garb, I feel sure I should not have fainted under the excitement of a haunting. Polly agrees. And that is the last, I think, that I shall say of that.

I rejoined my friend in his study. His man had clearly imposed some tidying effort upon Random as well, for he too was his perfectly appointed self: he took his sartorial notes from the Romantic poets, and the wild black curls lay momentarily tamed upon the shoulders of a long, black silk coat I took to be Egyptian. At least he was not wearing a fez.

As I entered, he stood and saluted me with a glass of his very fine claret. Bathed as he was in lamplight, I observed with

annoyance that Random Corwyn remained the handsomest man
of my acquaintance. Some days I wished he were fully my father's
age, so as to offer less distraction. Thankfully, my determination
to eschew the questionable joys of marriage for the sake of my
work has not been in any way altered by his charms.

Random put a glass of that excellent claret in my hand and a
chaste kiss on my cheek.

"You look just like a girl in that painting. Remember the
Rossetti we saw? Well never mind. But that color..."

"I do wish you wouldn't flirt. I am supposed to be your step-
sister."

It is what we give out to spare my reputation, and true enough
for the world's use. He laughed.

"You would not want me for a brother. I'm very hard on
siblings."

"You are hard enough on your friends!"

"Now who's flirting?"

"You are. And vulgar besides."

The billiard table that dominated the room was, as usual,
piled with books both closed and open, strange coins and bits of
curious jewelry, scrolls, maps and mysteries. Behind it in the
alcove under tall bay windows, a pair of padded wicker chairs
shared a tidy desk of Oriental design. Laughing, he guided me to
my usual seat, then took his own.

"Now tell me what is going on," I said.

"Of course," he said. "You want to know why I was so
unforgivably abrupt on your arrival," he said. "Yes?"

"Yes, and—"

"And why I threw you at once into the experiment with no
word of explanation."

"I think I know, but—"

"And you would know the source of my agitation. I who am
the most even-tempered of men."

"*Magister!*"

My glass came down firmly with a click. He only sipped at his wine, grinning at me over the rim, then sat back and began to tell the tale.

"The truth is, my dear pupil, that I sent for you because I wanted your very level head to confirm my observations, and I offered no explanation because I thought it best not to compromise your reaction. Also," he added rather quickly, "to test the equipment, which is new and uses in part galvanic energy to power it."

I stared at my left hand recalling the tingle when I had first touched the metal box. As I am well accustomed to being his test subject, I merely frowned.

"The device allowed me, I hope, to take an imprint of your experience, all of it, so that I can compare it to mine. I think I spoke of it the last time you were here."

"Yes."

"I shall give it further study later on, but I already know that you and I shared the same sort of vision, although different in some significant ways. For example, I saw the mottled light, and the young girl you described. But I also felt another intelligence behind it, which you did not. But though it reached for me, it drew back. Perhaps because I am so much more fearsome than you are." A slight smile twitched the corners of his mouth, and he lifted graceful hands. "Who can say?"

That was not the reason, and I felt he knew what it was, or suspected, but had no intention of telling me. There is much about himself that Random Corwyn keeps secret, though tantalizing clues sometimes drop from him as a joke or a sudden silence that means he is not telling the entire truth. He never lies, of that I'm sure, but prevarication is second nature to him.

"And the sadness?"

He nodded. "I felt it, yes, but not I think so deeply as you. A woman's despair is not like a man's."

"It took me by surprise," I said, a touch defensively. "Do you know who she is, the ghost girl? It is a ghost, is it not?"

"Let me tell you what I know. And I should begin by saying that I had been away on other business for several weeks when it all began."

Now he spoke as one hurrying past a graveyard. There was much to tell and none of it pleasant.

"You remember the Reverend Mr. Mayhew, I expect—the vicar of the church in the village?"

"He has never entirely approved of me."

"I shall introduce him to my lord the bishop, your father."

"He doesn't entirely approve of me, either," I answered dryly

Random acknowledged that with a lifted eyebrow. "Anyway, I had returned no more than a day before the vicar called upon me in great distress, with a face as long as a bass viol and a dreadful tale, which I believe is related to both our visions. You see, a fortnight since, Mr. and Mrs. Mayhew lost their daughter, their only child, a girl of twelve or so. There is an old well in the wood above the common, and sometime after the Sunday service, the girl—Helen, she's called—took it into her head to make a wish, or so her friends report. Now children hereabouts are firmly taught never to go into the fairy wood, as they call it, so of course they dare each other regularly, which may be what happened though none of them will own to it. When she had not returned by Evensong, everyone was frantic. All the village turned out to search with torches and dogs, but found no sign. By morning, they had persuaded themselves that she was away with the faeries, and they all went home to mourn and pray."

"Faeries? Do you think that likely?"

I have never encountered the sort of faery that people carry on about—tiny winged creatures dining on dewdrops. But there is no question that many of the uncanny creatures we encounter in our work are denizens of the domain which Random calls Faerie.

His lips creased in a thin, knowing smile. "I've never known that wood to be anything but perpetually damp, and rather pretty in a mossy, misshapen way. Rocky slopes and perilous footing are your fate if you stray from the narrow path—like the road to heaven, as the vicar would say. At its center is a clearing with, what... a low cave covered with brambles to hide a family of foxes, and the small spring that feeds St Wilgyth's well. The maidens used to tie wishes in the whitethorn bush when Wilgyth was just a wood nymph, and a while after that, too. Bluebells and primroses bloom all summer there."

I could not help but smile. "You know it well, then. It sends you to poetry."

"Eh? Not so well as all that, but I know it has no evil reputation. Folk who wander in usually wander out again soon enough. The local people avoid it out of what they call courtesy to their good neighbors, not for fear of goblins."

I suppressed a shudder, recalling my first encounter with goblins. I will never look at cheese the same way again.

"A cave, a spring, and a crystal well mark the place where spirits dwell," I said, mostly to myself.

"Indeed," he continued, "and yet that was where her father found her, alive but deeply unconscious in the mouth of that cave, half hidden by the undergrowth. She was dressed only in the muddy rags of her petticoats. Her arms and legs were bruised and bitten; her feet torn and bloody. He managed to carry her as far as this house, where Mrs. Jenkins looked after her for a day or two. The ridiculous local medico spun some absurd story about Helen larking about the common taunting the sheep until the dogs attacked her. Pure mischance, he said, and her own fault. Bled her a little, of course, since that's all he knows how to do when there are no bones to set, and took his fee."

"You do not agree," I suggested. He is always scornful of physicians.

"I do not. I've seen the girl, and even now the hurts are too extensive. More likely she was run round and round the mulberry bush, chased through that wood by something which thought it entertaining to torment a child."

"Dear God, Random, you never told her father that!"

"My dear girl, of course not," he said with a small sigh. "I'm told that, once in her own bed, she regained a degree of consciousness, but alas, her wits had fled. They could get no sense from her nor any hint what had truly happened. From that moment, she slept each day away until nightmares should wake her with screaming. Her mother would sing an old nursery song often used in their family, which brought her some peace whilst it continued. But as soon as the song stopped, she fell to weeping until overcome by sleep. The parents were quite beside themselves, as you can imagine."

At this he leaned cross the desk, hands clasped, and lowered his voice. "Now, all that might simply be a rural tragedy, but for what happened next."

Then he smirked when I jumped just the tiniest bit at a servant's quick double-knock at the study door.

"Enter," he called. One of the footmen came in and apparently asked if he should make up the fire and light the lamps, though I never heard a word between them, and saw only the master's slight nod. To me he said, "You're trembling, Miss Delacourt. Your heart is racing. You want to deal with that."

It's true my hands were cold. I had supposed it a relic of the encounter, or simply a consequence of Ransom's chilling story, but the room had indeed become quite icy as we talked. A light summer rain had begun pattering, and a fire would be welcome. Mrs. Jenkins came in as well to bring a plate of freshly baked gingersnaps and say goodnight, unless she was needed, though she knew very well that she was not. She's a plain old thing, brown as a gypsy, and devoted to Random as all his household are. Her bread and cakes are the talk of the county, and she beamed when I mentioned it.

The trembling stopped as I warmed a little, but he was right. Listening to his story as the evening deepened to night, I had naturally opened myself to the gift that Ransom is pleased to call, without irony, my intuition. I have learnt that if I am to rely upon it, I must find and cling to a balance between controlling my emotions and accepting them. Too much control cripples the gift; too little sweeps it away. My trembling fingers had showed Random what I had missed: the tale had been so affecting, and so soon upon the heels of a paraphysical encounter, that I had lost that balance. I had best collect myself before the next one.

My friend, who is never either too cold or too warm, as far as I can tell, poured us each another glass of wine while the footman went about his business. When the fellow finally bowed and left, Random took up the tale without insulting me by checking my hands.

"There is more. The night before last, the vicar woke to find the night winds rushing through his house, slamming doors and throwing ornaments down from the walls."

"A poltergeist?"

"Ah, no, more's the pity. He hurried downstairs carrying his old fowling piece to find his front door standing wide open to the elements. When he stepped outside hoping to catch an intruder, a strange wailing drew him into the garden. What he found there was Helen with all her limbs tangled in a thorn bush as if she had been thrown through it. She was covered in deep scratches, and streaming blood." A pause to sip his wine. "And she was singing."

Already horrified, my stomach lurched. "Singing?"

"He went to free her, of course, but before he could lay a hand on her, she stared up at the moon, what last sliver was left of it. She let out the most heart-rending moan, then went still."

A deep shudder shook me from head to toe, which I governed at once. "So, she is dead?"

"No, and you see, that's the odd thing." His eyes at last met mine through the firelight. "She's the only one who isn't."

"Only one? I don't understand. Then what is the ghost?"

"Is it a ghost?"

The uncharacteristic agitation of the afternoon returned with similar intensity. It flung him out of his chair like a black bird exploding into flight. The lamplight seemed to find him even as he sorted through the piles on the billiard table, shuffling papers, tossing aside a modern novel. With a sharp cry, he pounced upon a packet and returned to me, fairly shimmering with restrained passion. He sat with a sigh, and threw down a series of pictures.

"These are the others. Four that we know of since Helen was discovered."

"So many!" I laid them out before me like divining cards: homely photographs or tintypes of somber, stiffly posed family groups not daring to smile lest they be thought frivolous. And in each one, no matter how many children ranged about their parents, no matter how old the picture, I knew at once which of them was our ghost's victim. Each one all but shouted at me from the paper.

"This is not the work of a ghost or a faery."

"It is not. Now they are saying a demon creeps about at night to murder their children, but I can see nothing that has happened to draw a demon here."

"What then? Some kind of animal?"

"A wolf, perhaps? No, a wolf kills to eat, not for pleasure. These children have all been spirited from their homes by night, then killed in the wild, their wretched bodies left to the elements."

"Then what did we see? Surely that was her spirit. What sort of ghost can possess another?"

"Would you know that face again if you saw it?" he asked.

I nodded, and took the last picture from him, this one flushed with hand-tinted color. It showed a stiff, small schoolgirl sitting primly on a hard chair, with a vast ribbon bow perched on her long fair hair. A hint of mischief looked out of the pale blue eyes of a child who would cheerfully pursue a whim up a woodland path against her parents' command.

"This is Helen!" I could not have been more certain. "A little younger, but the same girl, without question. But how—"

"I can't say. She has fallen into a coma."

"What if," I wondered slowly, "her spirit is wandering? What if this second spirit has trapped her, is using her somehow to— I don't know, to attract the others?"

"All right, but to what end?" I felt his anger flare. "What has brought it here where such a creature has never been? Oak and Ash! It's maddening! This manor is my domain. I am responsible for these people, and their children."

I could not tell him not to be foolish, but I did say, "You have been reading Sir Walter Scott again, haven't you? Very romantic."

But it wasn't that simple; the outrage stemmed not from some idealized notion of a himself as a benevolent feudal lord caring for his simple, happy peasants. Such fancies are all too easily set aside when no longer amusing or convenient. Random Corwyn meant what he said. He spared no patience for questions without answers, only for unravelling the paraphysical tangle.

"I wonder," I said slowly. "The world has changed so much and so swiftly, and England more than anywhere. With every new mill or factory, how many uncanny creatures must be displaced, both dark and light? It almost makes me sad."

That appeared to amuse him. "Pity the poor monster with no black and foetid pool to lurk in? You're not usually so sentimental."

"And you're not usually so cynical. What does happen to them? Where do they go?" He shrugged lightly, so I went on. "I propose that a congenial, country parish lagging behind the times, might seem ideal to an uprooted spirit. Especially if its pool has been drained and dredged to build a factory, or its wood cut down for cheap new houses. Streams diverted, mines cut, canals... No, not a canal, I think, or we would see drowning. Drowning?"

"None." He was starting to look more interested as I set out my ideas. "All savaged by something with terrible claws, but not drowned."

"Not Peg Powler or one of her sisters, then. Not a kelpie, nor a beckhast. Whatever it is, I believe it must be very angry, even vengeful. It cannot punish the folk who displaced it, but ours will do."

At this, Random cocked his head like a curious raven, intrigued.

"Routed out by the iron tools of Man, eh? Yes, it's possible. Mrs. Jenkins says that some in the village claim to have seen Helen at night riding an enormous black dog by moonlight. One mother swears she saw her standing at the garden gate and pointing at her house. The next day, her child was gone."

"Random, what if she did?"

"What?"

"The mother. What if her story is not mere hysterics. We must consider that this thing is using Helen, riding her, as you said. That poor mother may well have seen some kind of manifestation of Helen's spirit in company with the creature. A bargest, maybe. A bargest, or a boggle, takes the shape of a black dog, among other things."

He considered this, nodding. "As can several others of that sort. You have been studying, I perceive. Very well, but there was no dog in either of our apparitions."

"Some other shape-shifter, then."

"Who can also possess or control a living human being."

"Yes."

"How to be rid of it, then?"

His thought was already away. Most times, no matter the challenge—whether quelling a dark witch, laying revenant ghosts, or revealing a hoax—he treats it as a game, keeping both a light heart and a scathing wit throughout. When the very old or the very young are made victims, the paraphysical explorer's charming, scholarly detachment grows thin.

Staring into the fire, he said, "My neighbors have decided, in that astonishing way humans have of leaping to conclusions out of fear, that the source of the evil is Helen herself, because she is mad, and because she lives though the rest have died. I'm told they are saying that Helen Mayhew must have sold herself to the Devil in that wood. They fear she is a witch, and want her tried, and hanged. That's why I sent for you, my dear—to temper my despair with this so-called enlightened age, or any age of Man."

He spoke of humans so coldly: I shivered at how his words separated him from the rest of us. In a way, I understood the desire not to be associated with the family into which we all are born, unthinkable though it was. Then his other words sank in.

"Random Corwyn, you will not let them hang that child as a witch!"

At the fireplace he stood a black silhouette rimmed with fire, almost shimmering not only from the firelight, but as if he might wink out of existence at any moment. This was the form of his anger, seldom seen and all the more terrible for its singularity.

I reached out, hesitated, drew back. In this state he is not entirely safe, to himself or to the furniture. Words are better, music better still to restore order to his chaos, to restore him to himself.

So I sang to him a verse he had taught me, a key he called it. Both the tune and the words are essential to its efficacy; the words are the greater challenge as they are strange, and awkward to pronounce, and must be kept in the heart, never written down. Roughly, they translate thus:

> *What shall we do, then?*
> *We shall master the light.*
> *Let us fly the path.*
> *Be one with the dance.*

One day, perhaps, I will understand their meaning, but for now it was enough to sing.

Breathless moments passed. The flame of his passion became a low glow I could almost see as he brought it under control. My eyes were glistening when his fists relaxed open. With care he touched cool fingers to my wrist, and I breathed more easily.

'Thank you, wise Violet." Random roused himself, and said, "Well, now that you know the whole tale, and the stakes, let us look again at this apparition."

ii

The day had begun for me many hours before, and I was close to yawning even if Random never seemed to tire. "I shall want a strong pot of tea after this, mind you."

He smiled, "Of course."

"Or brandy."

"I'm sure that can be arranged."

"Then I will try."

I took one last taste of the claret, this time filling my mouth with wine rather than sipping daintily; this time savoring the grape within the complex flavors; feeling the tannin almost cinnamon as it slipped down my throat; and the dark warmth. Choosing comfort, I arranged myself and several yards of embroidered skirt in one of the wing chairs nearest the hearth and leaned back, thankful for the fluid nature of my sensible (but beautiful) clothing. More daring still for a maiden lady, or any lady, I kicked off my slippers, tucked my stockinged feet up under me, and let myself sink into the scents and textures of the leather taut under my hands, the cloud-like silk, the fine linen nearest my skin fragrant with jasmine. From these sensations all my senses rose, and where such pleasures might have been soporific, I was energized. All weariness dismissed, I called upon my gift.

From the stillness of the balance point itself, I let spring open the gates Random had helped me to build, gates to keep the disorderly fragments of life from overwhelming me as they used to do. I willed them to flow, connect, and interact, to form associations and patterns. I had been collecting data since the raven's feather came to me so many hours ago. I had listened and watched. Now it all rose to my conscious mind, first as the lacy ghosts of things and thoughts, of faces and voices, and then... I frowned. Something was missing. How was that possible? The day's haphazard, unsorted moments ought to have been forming coherent phrases, palpable and measured. Measured!

"Random?" I said carefully without looking up. "What music did you play for me this afternoon? What sort of tune?"

"Nothing, I don't know." He sounded puzzled. "Just improvising, I think. I stopped when you cried out. Why?"

"But I heard it the whole time. Can you play it now, please—only this time, change the key. Or no, change from minor to major. And louder, much louder!"

"Violet, why are you shouting?"

"What?"

A great wind was roaring in my ears, in my mind, tumbling my images with the whistling fury of a storm at sea, the massed gallop of charging horses, or the scream of a woman in pain, a child's cry. The creature, not merely my memory of it, had already found me. I felt it tear at my barriers, pluck at my fears to throw them back at me. All the while, armed with only half-formed ideas, I could but stand, Horatius at the bridge, holding off the assault armed only with cool reason. I cringed against the blast but my training and my heart held true.

Then through the roar, the sobbing voice and the stab of despair suddenly altered, calmed by the lilting almost-human voice of the Stradivarius. Last time, plaintive; this time merry; though the notes might have been the same, they lifted the heart and set it dancing.

Be one with the dance, I thought.

In the face of such buoyant good cheer, the raging stilled. Young Helen's spirit, or her image, emerged out of the billowing cloud, hollow-eyed, weighed down with the reek of dead flowers. Then I saw it, the hint, the shadow I had missed before.

I sat straight up, not trusting myself to stand. "Who are you?"

"What do you see?" Random asked.

"The other spirit, the true ghost. She is there, can't you see her?" I grabbed his bow hand and clasped it near my heart to share the vision. "Show thyself, spirit, I command thee!"

A long groan answered, low as a bass viol's bottom note, and rose through the orchestra until it burst into an hysterical, inhuman cackle. Helen's terrified face folded in on itself and winked out, leaving the other entity exposed. In whatever space it occupied, on whatever plane, the pale figure of a gentlewoman in the silk and lace of two and a half centuries ago floated semi-transparent against the gloom she had brought with her. In the remnants of an unearthly wind, her ringleted hair lifted along with the slashed ribbons of the once fine gown. For a moment she struck a pose of noble lamentation, one hand at her breast, then her face changed, and her attitude, like an actress dropping character. She seemed confused at first, then joyfully held out her arms and welcomed into them a swarm of small swirling lights. I knew at once what lights those were.

"Who are you?" I demanded. "What do you want?"

"The children. Only the children. Young Helen, too—let her come to me."

"We do not keep her, spirit. She lives. It is for you to let her go."

"You are cruel to stay her when she is in such pain."

Random, who both saw and heard her now quite plainly, if his grim looks meant anything, spat his disbelief.

"Cruel? When it is you have driven her mad? When her pain is all of you?"

Slowly, the apparition turned its imperious gaze, then dismissed him and returned to me with another voice, very different: wheedling and scornful together with curious notes of the North.

"Come with us, human child! The faery princeling cannot love you." (I felt him stiffen beside me.) *"Forsake your tedious books, your unwomanly ambitions. We shall be forever free of care."*

A lady does not snort with laughter, so that vulgar noise cannot have been mine. Rather, I sneered, "What, to spend eternity with *you?* You do not know me, spirit. And there is nothing in you but ignorance and death. Now tell me your name."

But it had no intention of putting such ammunition into our hands. It only repeated, *"Come with us, little Violet! Come play or come die!"*

"Enough!" It was too much for my friend. "In the name of God, be gone!"

The baleful light snapped out, though the terrible figure's image remained on my eyes, counterchanged, even as it vanished.

Blinking, deeply exhausted, I wanted to fall back into the chair, lay down my head, rest but I dared not. I had opened to the world; I needed to close in. So I forced myself to look about, to focus on particular things: to see my friend's sharp, attentive features; to hear rain tapping at the glass, and smell the wood fire spicy on the hearth, feel the spike of its warmth. Gently, Random wrapped my hands around the heat of an exquisite bone china cup of tea that I hadn't known was there, fragrant with cinnamon and orange peel. The solidity of even such a dainty thing, the sweet and bitter flavors on my tongue, confirmed to me that my senses had returned to the plain reality of the mortal world.

"Well," I said when I had caught my breath and reclaimed my *sang-froid.* "That was—interesting. I had not expected her to be dismissed so easily!"

But it was only temporary, as Random reminded me. Ghost or demon, they recoil from that simple exhortation, but are not vanquished by it.

My friend, who as usual was not tired at all, had turned up one of the lamps and taken it across the room to a glass-topped case, where he stood frowning at a collection of old miniatures. "Who was she, I wonder. And what is using her? And how?"

"You felt that too, then? There was another voice, wasn't there? A *third* voice. What in Heaven's name is going on?"

Tight-lipped, uncommonly perplexed, he shook his head. "I wish I knew. Tell me, lady scholar, what sort of boggle can do all this?"

He slid out the tray of the display case and removed one of the tiny portraits to consider it more closely. "On the other hand..."

"On the other hand?" I prompted, and this time a yawn came over me whether I would or no.

"On the other hand," he repeated, slipping the *bijou* into a pocket with a wry grin, "the world is full of things I do not know."

"Many?"

"A few."

"You astonish me, sir. Why did it call you a faery princeling?"

I registered the hint of a small smile, but he said only, "I can't imagine."

"But..."

"You may find this interesting."

He plucked up a small book from the table, apparently hand-bound in a carved wooden cover to which a kind of lock had been fixed. A breviary, perhaps, or a diary.

"There was a sort of small monastery here once, you know, very early on."

I hazarded a guess. "Dedicated to St Wilgyth?"

"Of course. And one of the monks, a Brother Osbert, seems to have been a natural observer, rather like you. He certainly kept his wits about him, and even wrote some brief, uneasy reports. Listen to this:

> *Brother Gwyn having been attacked by a wild beast*
> *died after Matins. He is the third of our number so*
> *afflicted. The beast cannot be found. Some say it is*
> *invisible, being a thing from Hell. It is now said that*
> *some devil liveth by the spring in the bluebell*
> *wood. I have warned my brothers not to stray*
> *there, but the path is easy and the water sweet.*
> *Thus is ever Satan's way.*

"Tempted by the easy path, as always. And further on, here it is, he says

> *Bishop Cuthbert came to us and a Mass was sung*
> *in the moss wood where we dedicated the spring*
> *there to the blessed Wylgytha that was our abbot.*
> *The enemy of God flew out at the Elevation of the*
> *Host. When the preaching was done, the brothers*
> *departed, then the demon returned to defy him.*
> *Next day, the bishop strove again with the demon.*
> *He burned him with an iron rod. On the third day,*
> *the bishop —*

"What's this?

> *— rolled up his sleeves and—*

"Well, the text is blurred, but he seems to have prevailed, because next it says—

> *The bishop departed to Exeter and the people of*
> *God were no more assailed."*

"I thought the wood had no bad reputation!"
"Well it doesn't, now. A thousand years is a long time in the lives of men," he mused. "Long enough for a story to fade."

"Or perhaps it was only a wolf, as you said before, or a mad man. This monk knew a good story when he told one."

"Very likely," he said. That brought a knowing smile. "I say—Cuthbert; that's your excellent father's name, isn't it? Coincidence, I'm sure."

"Like the wood nymph and the saint?"

"Exactly. Though I suspect she had relocated by then."

Next thing I knew, he was blowing dust from a book not quite so ancient which he had plucked from a shelf behind me. Sometimes he moves as he thinks—so fast I half wonder if I have nodded off unknowing.

"Come along, Miss Delacourt. You have earned your whiskey. There is a decanter in the gallery, and a picture I wish to examine. And do bring the gingersnaps."

He flung back the heavy door as if it had no weight at all, evidently heading for the long gallery on the floor above. (Parts of the house are very old.) Weary though I was, I slipped back into my shoes before following at a more leisurely pace.

The gallery, as I'm sure you recall, is extraordinary, with Italianate plasterwork in the ceiling and other fine details beloved by antiquaries. In fair weather, the open side provides a view of the extensive gardens from an extravagance of mullioned windows. For the rest, portraits of other people's ancestors are gradually being replaced with misty landscapes, Pre-Raphaelite fantasies, and whimsical faery paintings. These last tickle Random excessively, especially if Queen Titania is featured, but he will never say why. That I have spent this time describing the room to you rather than his discovery tells you something of my state of mind and my memory of the moment.

In fact, I found him in front of an age-darkened portrait labelled *Laetitia, Lady Robert Beckwith (1605-1644)* and holding up the miniature for comparison. His eyes were brighter than ever. Mine, I noticed, were hot and filled with gravel.

"Found her!" Random barked in the quick, clipped manner he employs at mid-discovery. "I thought I knew her. Isn't she grand?"

Yes, there she was, the face and figure we had seen, though triumphant and glowing with abundant health. The anonymous artist had depicted her armed like Boadicea in a golden chariot, shaking her spear against the foe. I should perhaps have paid more notice to her charioteer, half hidden behind the Lady's flowing sleeve: a small, black-haired man of hideous aspect, his face and arms dark with Pictish spirals. But I was weary, and Random was speaking.

The book he had brought provided a gloss, how Lady Beckwith and her household had held Corbisend, or Corby's End as it was then, in the King's name for four days against Cromwell's troops, before being shamefully betrayed by a treacherous kitchen maid. When they were overrun, she and her children, well, they died there. Thankfully, the writer had drawn a veil across the manner of their deaths. The artist, working during the Restoration, had clearly used the miniature as the model for her face and generous bosom, but the rest was pure fancy.

I'm afraid that, while not unsympathetic with her plight or my friend's enthusiasm, I yawned like a country bumpkin, which shocked Random sufficiently to notice the case clock in the corridor striking midnight. It may be useful to recall that I had left Cambridge on an early train and arrived after supper. It had been a very trying day.

"You don't mean to say you're tired?" he asked.

I replied that even though he may thrive on little sleep, we ordinary mortals are not so blessed, or something of that sort.

Polly was called, as drowsy as I, to unpin my hair and locate my nightdress, and put me to bed at last between crisp embroidered linens. The light rain had stopped, so I had her push the unlatched windows open to the balmy night. She frowned her disapproval. Everyone knows, and Polly is ever quick to remind me, that open windows permit noxious airs and worse to enter and infect the sleeper. Also thieves, murderers, and flies. But Random has persuaded me that country air, particularly at Corbisend, is a tonic, and I have always felt well there, except when I was injured.

That night I slept almost before my head touched the pillow.

iii

Was I dreaming when she came to me, Lady Laetitia Beckwith? I think not, for if it was but a dream then nothing that came after makes any sense at all. Does that serene balance point between passion and cool reason persist even in sleep?

A headache woke me at some deep hour when even the owls have caught their mice and gone home to bed. Save for the ordinary creaks and pops common to old buildings, the house stood in utter silence. Only the candle at my bedside gave any light. Still, something had changed, or was changing.

And then I saw her, a white mist at first that formed in a corner near the ceiling and grew as if descending a staircase though no staircase stood there now. I sat up shivering with cold but unafraid, the trained observer, and watched as mist took shape from the candlelight. At last the semi-transparent likeness of Lady Beckwith hovered just beyond the foot of my bed, and the air lightly touched with lavender and thyme. In one hand she held a ghostly candle, which she held up while bending slightly, crooning an almost familiar tune. The other hand reached down in a familiar petting gesture, unmistakably that of a mother caressing a child's hair while it sleeps.

After a moment, a few murmurous words, she moved on to repeat the action, and once more. So this room had been the nursery, once; those children long dead, were her children. When she was content that they slept well, the ghostly mother glided to the window where she stood for a while staring into the night.

Surely this apparition was a mere residual haunting, the echo of a real moment, unaware of me or the passage of time. It must have been repeating, spinning like a millwheel down the centuries, re-enacting a last moment of peace, perhaps, before the hobnailed boots of the soldiery tore their lives apart. I had never read or heard that such a *residuum* could be manipulated or copied. And if Lady Beckwith were only an echo, what had we seen before?

Slowly the eerie gaze turned in my direction.

"You must help us," she said in a voice nearly as smoky as her visage, though there was no mistaking the tone of command.

I jumped a bit, I admit it, then froze and waited, prepared to observe closely until the *residuum* faded away.

"Can you not hear me, mistress?"

Shocked into a gasp, I tried to speak, but though my lips moved, I am sure, no words came from them. Random would have said that I was clutching my gift to keep it from hiding under the bed.

"Help us, for pity!"

I managed a pathetic stammer, and watched her sorrow turn to scorn.

"I had expected more heart in a woman. Alas, I have made that mistake before."

She was speaking to me! No mere *residuum*, but truly present and aware, the candlelight glimmered on ghostly tears, and the lady began to dissipate. That finally moved me to action. I could not lose her.

"My lady, wait!" I cried. "Pray do not go. I will help you, only I do not know how."

The image ceased retreating and took on color and some slight substance. Swiftly I threw on my shawl, then I climbed out of bed and curtsied as deeply in my nightdress as I did to the Archbishop in my best gown. She blinked, and waited.

I said, "Dear Lady Beckwith, my name is Miss Violet Delacourt. I am a—well, we call it a paraphysical observer. Pray tell me what has happened to you, and I will listen."

The courtesy, the acknowledgement of her station seemed to have calmed her, and she began to tell her tale. To my abiding relief, the Lady Beckwith remained as forthcoming in death as she had been in life, though her narrative drifted easily into tears and self-recrimination. Born near Wakefield, Laetitia Simson had come a young bride to this great southern house, leaving all her family behind...

Unfortunately I had not yet learned how best to interrogate a ghost so as to elicit only the relevant information and not an entire history. In the end, with some gentle nudges and much repetition, the details unfolded.

I will spare you that sorry tale, both to save your patience and because I may one day compose a novel around it. What was useful for us to know was that she haunted Corbisend seeking her babes who perished here, as she had herself, after surrendering the house to one of Cromwell's generals. Weightless and timeless, Lady Beckwith wept and wandered singing her melancholy song through sealed up doors and ruined cottages, as far as the old boundaries of the manor, including—you have guessed it—the faery wood and St Wilgyth's well.

"Go not to the well!" she warned again and again. "Beware the black dog."

Poor apparition! How her insubstantial self had been trapped or to what purpose she could not say, nor what sort of creature this monster was; it was not here in happier days. Her sense of time's passing was uncertain at best, but she confirmed that the spirits of the village's murdered children were, as I had thought, the little spark-lights that clung to her now like little clouds. She sang to comfort them, she told me. Again she begged me to let Helen's spirit come to her. Perhaps tomorrow, I said, for I knew not what else to tell her.

When I had learned all I could, I dared one final question, but as I feared, she knew nothing of Random Corwyn nor of faeries. The mocking voice had not been hers; it was not human, nor never was. Very well, I had enough to think about without such nonsense.

Her story done, the pauses grew longer, her distraction greater, until it was clear she had forgotten me. Gazing again out of the window across the starlit world, she murmured, "He will come too late, too late, too late."

A yawn overtook me but I watched as she resumed the same automatic motions as before, humming that familiar tune.

Quite suddenly, I sneezed. The air had changed again, the stench of rising damp driving out the fresh scent of herbs that had been her signature.

"Look where it comes!" Laetitia wailed. "We are lost!"

Pure cold washed in as if snow had filled the room, driving away the balmy summer night. Hoarfrost rimed the looking glass with Chinese fans, and my breath steamed. I saw icicles forming even on the candlesticks, as I sought shelter under the featherbed. Then the candle blew out. The shutters slammed shut *bang*! over every window.

Blinded, I cried out, "Who is there?"

In reply a deep, jolly voice rang out sending the chorus of a vulgar song bouncing off the linen-fold walls, countering and cancelling Laetitia's lullaby.

> *Singin' bide, lady bide!*
> *There's nowhere you can hide*
> *For the lusty smith will be your love*
> *And he will lay your pride!*

A low moan, a shriek in the darkness, and I knew she was gone before the song had finished. And when the voice had choked on its terrible laugh, a figure loomed out of the dark with a growl low in its throat. A enormous shaggy black dog, fully the size of a moor pony, stood but a few feet from me, outlined in its

own baleful light. Coarse fur bristled about a thick, bearlike neck.
Fiery eyes as big as saucers burned beneath dagger-pointed ears,
and a ditchwater reek came from its foul mouth. My stomach
lurched in disgust.

I blinked; the dog vanished, and in his place stood a small,
squint-eyed manikin, his pale green skin pricked out in blue
designs, the image of Queen Boadicea's barbaric charioteer.

"Whoop!" he cried and vaulted over the bed, spun about, and
came down in a coat of green velvet and silk knee britches, with a
gold-laced cocked hat on his head. The same fiery eyes shone out
of a face as horrible as the black dog's. He danced a jig step or two
and bowed over his hand.

"Well met, little maiden. Sweet Violet, sweeter 'an t' roses!"

The sneering voice had been raked over the slagheap of some
bleak Northern coal pit. I may perhaps be forgiven for trembling
in the face of it. And yet for all that, the observer remained awake,
and the half-trained magician. I gulped back the bitter stuff in my
mouth, and my will held.

"What are you?" I demanded more boldly than I felt. "Why
do you torment this village?"

"Why, because I can! Because it pleases me to stir up the
mortal folk for my amusement, dead or alive."

"Why torment Helen? Why entrap Laetitia?"

"Ha-ha-ha, my girl!" he cackled as he hopped about like Tom-
Tit-Tot. "It is my revenge on 'em doing me out of hearth and
home, and of my entertainment. That is the price of sending me
packing! I was their luck, now I shall be their misfortune."

"Theirs?"

"Theirs! Yours! All of your greedy kind, and the raven boy,
too, and you. I have done them all. I shall do you, too. *Whoo
hoo!*"

My thoughts assembled even as he skipped and bounced
from floor to chair to dressing table, punctuating his words with a
smashed mirror, a thrown pincushion. I had to duck more than

once, so my gift may have been out of tune due to the hairbrush bouncing painfully off the bone of my wrist, but even in the chaos, several clues resolved.

The more rustic places of our island are known for a type of household spirit, mischievous and helpful by turns, which may sometimes become so attached to a family that even through the generations, it will not leave. All the stories tell how unshakeable they are; not one that I knew of told how one could be got rid of, or the goblin it becomes when its heart turns cold. Some scholars assume that if the family is extinguished, so too is the creature. Others say it becomes twisted and grows dark, a wretched boggart haunting abandoned places and lonely roads, tormenting travellers. What might such a one do when towns become cities, and abandoned farms give way to commerce and iron industry? The faerie kind cannot bear the touch of cold iron. Might it not seek out some remnant of the family it once served, wherever it might be?

I cried out, "I know what you are, Boggart!"

That made him stop cold on the floor, and when I blinked, he had become the image of Lady Beckwith in a green gown. It fixed the same fiery eyes on me as the little man, as the dog, with the same sharp teeth in its grin.

The creature said, all the more terrible for a sweet voice: "Do ye indeed? Knowing spares no porridge, maiden. The boy will not save you, little maid! No hero, he. And you shall be my next, next, next!"

"Think you so?" I said firmly. "I shall be my own hero, then."

Sheer bravado that was, though I did raise my hands to focus my will. I chanted, "Sheep-crook and black dog—"

But before I could say more, that black dog had leapt upon the bed, bearing me over with its great paws. I screamed, but only once, for his massive weight stopped my breath. I thought it had stopped my heart! Heavy claws raked my shoulder. I managed to gasp out a few words, but they were not enough. Jaws dripping, it roared in my face, and would have struck.

I screamed, "Random!"

The room lit up like daylight, and he was there, laughing and shining like a star. With a casual lift of his hand, the shutters flew open, warmth flooded in.

"What's all this then?" Random asked lightly. "Ah, you see, this is what comes of having pets on the bed."

The hound swung its heavy head round, growling in confusion.

"'Tis enough, *Scucca!*" He snapped its ancient name and smacked it hard with something that might have been a carriage whip or merely a hazel rod tipped with black iron. "Get down, I say, ye laidly cur! Bad dog!"

The black dog yelped. Random snapped his stick again, and the boggart sprang away snarling through the windows. As the dazzling light around me quickly faded, my rescuer went about lighting each lamp with a touch, and I sat up gasping.

"Here, drink this," he said at last. He handed me a crystal goblet and sat down beside me. "Are you all right?"

I nodded, and downed cool water with something sweetly herbal in it, refreshing, even healing.

It is never his habit to say what a brave girl I am, any more than he would have done to Peter. Nor does he try to hush away my fears, as one does with a child. So you should not be offended that he made no such gestures. He simply passed his hands over the cuts and bruises, rested longer where the heavy claws had scored lines of fire into my shoulders, and gave me time to collect myself. As my breathing calmed, I gave him my report without waiting to be asked. I told him what I have just told you about Laetitia and the creature, and my thoughts about them both. He did say "Well done," and meant it. What grimly pleased him best of all was the creature's confession and its threats. When I asked him why, he smiled.

"We don't need to wait for it to strike again. We know what it is, thanks to you, and we have its address."

In short order, and without disturbing the rest of the household, I was tucked up into another chamber, the windows latched. I fell asleep to the sound of his voice, and others higher and lighter, singing a stately antiphon of grace in the corners of the room until after the door had closed. Perhaps he set a charm upon the room, or on the house. Perhaps I already dreamed.

iv

In the morning, Polly refrained from asking me what had happened in the night and, not wanting to alarm her, I did not volunteer. The marks left by the attack had already faded though they itched a good deal, and my nerves had recovered with little mark upon them either. Experience, some would say stubbornness, has taught me quick recovery.

Random already occupied the morning room with coffee and the London newspapers, but he looked up at once when I came in. He scanned the practical costume I had chosen over Polly's objections, and raised an expressive eyebrow.

"If you've had your coffee and the London gossip, we should go," I said firmly. "My apologies to Mrs. Jenkins, but I could no more eat breakfast than I could lay an egg. No argument. We must rout this creature without delay."

Too late, I noticed he had already dressed in tweeds and boots, looking the perfect country squire. In fact he had folded and laid aside the *Times* before I had finished speaking.

"Indeed we must, my dear Miss Delacourt. You are quite right. "

"Well, then," I replied with a sniff. "Get your hat."

"Daniel!"

Captain Daniel Ford, who had served with us so well in Persia and elsewhere, came in to say that the horses were ready at the front door, awaiting our convenience. I suppose I will never learn.

Capt. Ford did not, by the way, did not so much as blink at the full-skirted Turkish coat I wore, even though it was not quite long enough to disguise the Turkish trousers beneath. Polly must have warned him.

Random asked dryly, "If we may pause for one logistical detail, *magistra*?" I'm afraid I rolled my eyes and sighed, which he took for permission. "Have you brought your revolver?"

"Of course," I replied, withdrawing it easily from my coat, which was blessed with numerous pockets and compartments. The revolver, a short-barreled .38-caliber Webley with handsome silver scrollwork and rosewood grips, slips into it admirably.

"Daniel, if you please?

The captain placed before me a box of cartridges and said, "We made these up specially for you, to Random's specification. They have an iron core for just such occasions."

"Since Persia?" I said, and opened the box at once.

"Since Persia was so nearly a disaster, yes. I do try to learn from my mistakes. Please reload with those and those alone. I'm sure I can contrive to bind and dismiss it, but if not?" The eloquent shrug. "It may be the only thing that will stop this creature."

Shortly we were mounted in the gravel drive, ready to set out. Random, who rides as he does everything else, with effortless grace, sat his glossy black hunter like a centaur. Perched side-saddle on the bay gelding, though somewhat less picturesque, I had no fear of keeping up with him. But before we could step away, Random pulled up sharply and dragged round the hunter's head, glaring down the slope and through the trees in the direction of the village.

Softly, he said, "Hark! The church bell is ringing."

A moment later, I head it too. "It is Sunday, Random. Of course it's ringing. My step-father will be cross."

"No, not that. Listen. It is the tolling bell. Damn it, I thought we had distracted it, but another child has died. And something else?"

"Yes."

The day had dawned warm and spicy, the rain clouds driven off by the habitual breeze that bent the gorse bushes and lifted a flock of crows into the air, circling and calling in the distance. Paper white and nearly full, the moon floated high in the western sky.

The lanes would yet be too damp to raise dust, but other sounds, a rustling movement along the hedges far below, came to me on a wave of potential action, as Random calls it. Listening to my gift, I understood a faint, rhythmic pattern in that wave to be a hurrying pony and trap.

"You have a visitor," I said. "Bringing trouble."

"Of course," said he, grinning fiercely. "Then let us ride to meet it."

He leapt away; I followed just as briskly across the deep lawns and so came to the main gates at a swift pace. There we found a middle-aged couple in their Sunday best, both looking frantic, rattling up to the gate.

"Mr. Corwyn!" the man sobbed, dragging back on the reins.

"Mayhew?" Random said. "What is the matter?"

"Mr. Corwyn, sir, for the love of God, you must help us!"

Random leant down and rested a hand on the man's shoulder, settling him enough to speak coherently, though the conversation remained curt and intense, questions and quick answers.

There are two of us for a reason. My attention went to the vicar's wife, her eyes red, the thin lips white with tension. In her arms she held an adolescent girl, painfully thin, bundled in a blanket. Even in her coma, the face was so familiar to me, I cried out.

"Helen!" It was a shock to realize I had never seen her in life until now.

"Aye?" said the vicar's wife, her frown deepening, for we had never met. "You meant my girl. Forgive me, Miss. That is my Christian name, as well, Helen Simson that was. You'd be his sister, then? Mr. Corwyn's step-sister?"

Hiding my shock at hearing her maiden name, I nodded and gave her my hand. Possibilities began to tumble through my mind.

"Forgive me if I seem to pry, Mrs. Mayhew, but it may help our efforts to know if you have any— It is far-fetched, I know, but— have you by chance any connections in Yorkshire?"

"What? Aye, you might say so." She eyed me doubtfully, drawing her child closer to her. I've seen that look more than once, but a gift must not be dismissed however faint.

I urged her to go on. "Family's all gone from there though. My granddad was born there, but he came here from the wars, one wet moor being good as any other, he said. Oh, Miss, I can hear them coming! You won't let your brother forsake my Helen, will you? I know men don't care much about a little girl. But a lady like yourself, Miss, you'll have kids of your own one day."

Her anguish was so great, I felt my own heart break with it. Twice now I had been begged by a mother for aid: I who never was a mother nor, by my intention, likely to be one. And yet the women's lot we all share bound me to them both, Laetitia and Helen, as surely as to my own mother.

"Not for all the world," I said. "Be assured of that."

Uncomforted, she clutched her husband's arm and burst into tears. "They are coming, Mayhew! Heaven spare us, they are coming! We cannot bide here. Please, oh please drive on!"

It was true, a mist of likelihood below us was growing, and the rumble of voices with it, some shouting, some swearing. My gift reached out for the new data swirling up with the noise. The church bell had not merely marked another child's death, it had been a call to arms, and the growing turmoil rose with the dust from the marching, shuffling feet of honest craftsmen and sturdy yeoman farmers pushed by the uncanny beyond their grace. In stopping to talk with us, the Mayhews had lost their lead.

"Nay, love," said the vicar, feigning calm for her sake. "Trust Mr. Corwyn. All will be well, you'll see. Mr. Corwyn will send them home."

I was impressed and gratified by their faith in my friend; he so often appears to be improvising. I only wished I were as certain. We had intended to face a boggart alone, unhampered by a mob of frightened, angry villagers.

"And here they are," Random drawled as the first of them came into view around the curve at the bottom of the hill. They must have just crossed the stone bridge. "Pitchforks. Mattocks. And torches!"

"In the daytime?"

"That doesn't bode well. Observe and record, please, Violet. Mayhew, behind me. Oh good, here's Daniel with the cavalry."

A small troop of Random's servants looking suspiciously like a household guard had just ridden up behind us. I was reminded that Captain Ford had commanded a troop in the Balkans. He reported with a sharp, "Sir?"

The orders were brief, efficient, and not for me. My focus was on the deep murmur along the road as it became a thudding rumble, and then a shout.

"In there!"

Riding forward a few steps, Random placed himself soberly at the head of our little party. "Stand fast, everyone, if you please," he said calmly.

There are times when he seems much older than his years, wise and sensible. Then there are moments like this when he has all the restraint of a wild young fellow when a dark gleam lights his eye.

It was almost comical when at last the mob surged through, a few dozen rude mechanicals waving agricultural implements, walking up each other's heels, blunt nose jammed suddenly into sun-reddened neck as they pressed between the stone gate posts, and found themselves brought up short not by a desperate little family with nowhere to run, but by the languid person of their landlord and his improbable sister. And half a dozen armed men. Almost comical, but not quite.

All fell silent when they registered who it was had halted their mad career, though a few grumbled. Most of them snatched off their caps, but a few stood firm, jaws set with grim determination. From the easy way he scanned their numbers, it was clear Mr. Corwyn knew them all by sight and probably by name, too.

"Well, Sam Shorland," he began, easily picking out the leader. "What is this all about?"

A big man with a bristling black beard, thewed like a chestnut tree, stood forward and planted himself, prepared to speak plainly.

"Beggin' yer pardon, Mr. Corwyn, sir, it's nowt to do wi' you. That girl's got a devil in 'er and it's killin' our kids. Now the Norris boy's taken, an' him just 'prenticed. We got no choice but to drive it out."

The rest joined their agreement with *Aye* and *Yes* and *So 'tis, squire!*

Another man raised his voice. "Mebbe she bain't no witch, that's more 'n we know, but I mind it be her at fault all the same. Her and the devil in that wood."

That is a sample of their speech, and enough transcription for patience. Shorland made his case that the witch girl and her demonic master must be destroyed, and they meant to do it and burn down the wood in which the monster lurked, no matter if Mr. Corwyn or Mr. Mayhew or God himself tried to stop them.

Random let the blacksmith carry on and as he spoke, the others, their indignation taking heart from his, began to voice their agreement, the fear and anger plain on their plain honest faces. Pitchforks and hoes began to shake in calloused fists, threatening mayhem.

Mr. Corwyn silenced them with a lifted hand and a short word, then turned in the saddle. Behind him, the vicar trembled, but rose when he was bidden, standing awkwardly in the rocking two-wheeled trap while the pony fidgeted.

"Go on, Reverend," he said gently. "Your turn."

Mayhew gulped, and essayed to speak.

"Friends!" he croaked, a horrible sound from the man charged with the cure of their souls.

They responded with a babble of shouting, but this time the blacksmith bellowed, "Let him talk!"

"Thank you, I— I have prayed for your children. All of our children. I— Oh God, can you not see Helen is bewitched? She is only a little girl like yours, Nellie Nesbit, or yours, Frank Digby."

But she wasn't the same, and they told him so. Their children were dying, the whole district lived in sleepless dread, while the vicar's girl not only lived but had been seen with the demon, choosing the victims.

It got worse, as a mob must. Other voices, other notions, turned pain to hysterics. Maybe the vicar himself was the witch. He was, and the whole family supped nightly with the devil himself! Their pain compounded, and someone remembered what their old granddad used to say was the only thing to do wi' a witch. And as the shared passion fed itself, they saw God's justice was out of balance and they themselves were born to right it.

"See the flames on 'im! There's the fires of Hell in the vicar's eyes!"

"I see it! Oh Jesus spare me, 'tis true!"

"The woman, too!"

It was too much. The dam broke. The loudest shoved forward to get at Mayhew and pull him down. One clambered onto the cart, clawing at Mrs. Mayhew and the girl, but all this was no part of Random's plan.

At his signal, one of his own men grabbed the pony's bridle and started to ride away, while others dragged off the attackers.

Daniel himself tried briefly to remove me from the scene, but I gave him such a look that he broke off right quick, as they say. Grinning, he touched his hat to me, and turned to send the Mayhews and three men galloping break-neck to the house. That done, he took his position at our backs while the remaining "footmen" used the flat of their blades, so I am assured, to restore order and quell any attempt to pursue. A few heads were cracked, but not many.

"You can't keep her, sir," the blacksmith's stentorian voice rose out of the hubbub, "without you put your whole house in danger as well as the village. What happens when the black dog comes to your door, eh, and one of your folk is next."

"Enough!" said Random Corwyn. The irresistible ring of command in his voice silenced them and somehow gathered them in.

"Listen, all of you. You all know me. Now, I've seen the newspapers and pamphlets handed round the Green Man, where they call me a magician, and a paraphysicalist. I know you've heard how on occasion we have banished ghosts and monsters that trouble honest folk just like yourselves, even across the sea."

Yes, they agreed, they knew it. They were proud of him, too, being their own. But here, amazingly, his tone altered. He was almost laughing as he asked:

"Do you think I would let my own people suffer?"

I thought it a mad question to ask of men in this mood. But he knew them so much better than I. They thought about it, and they looked at the ground and fiddled with their buttons, muttering, "No sir, no, of course not. Hardly that, sir."

"Will you trust me, then, eh?"

He went on to assure them that he and I, his lovely assistant, had the tools and the skills to take care of the trouble, and would do so. As for the vicar, he said with an edge of fatherly disappointment, they should be ashamed of themselves. If they had hanged that girl or drowned or burnt her in their anger and fear, however would they face each other again? How do business together, pray together ever afterwards, knowing what they had done? There would be no hiding who was involved in such savagery, especially when it failed to bring about the desired end, and the horrors continued.

Then he appealed to them as neighbors, as Englishmen, to let him—us—take care of this. It was most heartfelt, and it seemed to work on the men.

Nellie Nesbit and her gossips, though, weren't having any. She stood her ground with her fists on her hips, and said, "What're you going to do, then, Mister Corwyn?"

I expected that to stall him, however temporarily, but I should have known better. The mood had already lightened, and he had an advantage to press. So he did.

"Well, we are not going to burn down the wood, for starters!"

He said it in such a way as to make them laugh nervously at themselves. If I'm right, a vivid image came to all of them at once—and to me as well—of a conflagration fueled by that ancient wood sweeping down to the village and engulfing all their homes and the rest of their children, their parents, their lives, before even the greatest magician could stop it. How clear it was that it had only been talk; they'd never meant any such thing; who would do such a thing?

How Random did that trick, I do not know, but without answering their questions it brought his point home to the men. The little circle of women, however, tough country girls all huddled in their iron-red cloaks, stood shaken, silent, and unsatisfied.

The lesson ended, he solemnly enjoined them all to go back down to the church, or to go home, and pray and let us get on with our work. Chastened, they nodded. Some came up to shake Mr. Corwyn's hand before they left. Some he spoke to for a moment. Sam the smith he invited to come with us, a witness, he said. Frank Digby, too, whose cooperage sat across the river from the Green

Man inn, which he also owned. Random asked each a couple of quiet questions, then sent them to Daniel.

I was about to query his plans myself when I realized that nearly everyone had wandered off, or found a new task, but not Nellie Nesbit. That sturdy dyer, spots of accidental scarlet dashed though her fair hair, stood alone in the muddy track, worrying the corners of her Sunday best apron. When she looked at me, I smiled, but the grey eyes took in my notoriously unfeminine dress and turned swiftly away. But the men hadn't noticed her, and if she wasn't prepared to speak to me, what could she do? Finally she simply took a great breath and announced to the universe, or to God, or to the filthy creature waiting in the wood:

"Just so as you lads all know, I mean to come with you. To the wood, I mean."

Random Corwyn looked around, grinning as if he had known all along. "Of course you do," he said. "There ought to be one level head among us."

As he had not for the men, my friend dismounted and took her shaking hands and stilled them. Speaking low, he caught and held her with those wonderful eyes, and gave her heart, or instructions, or apologies, I knew not what. She brushed away a tear or two, and nodded. He kissed her cheek, and then he sent her to Daniel.

For as often as he appears to set himself outside the race of Man, sometimes in sorrow and often in arrogance, yet he has a caring soul.

"Very well, then," he called, swinging back into the saddle. "Miss Delacourt, at your convenience."

And we set off. The others we left with Daniel.

V

The music betrayed me. We rode first to the common, where a man and small white dog had brought a half-dozen sheep to graze in the wide swath between the wood and a reed-fringed pond. Little Helen had started here and so must we, though wiser and better armed. Whatever called her up the path that ran beside the little brook, I opened myself to it.

Nothing. Perhaps the time of day was wrong, the sun too high, the grass too wet, who could say. If it slept, we would wake it.

A quick-running stream emerged from the trees overarched by a tunnel of sighing trees, the greens of summer filtering the light that fell dappled to the path.

"How wonderful!" I breathed, and we rode in.

Any almanac will tell you that by mid-June, the bluebells should have been finished for the year, but here they were. Waves of blue and green like Persian carpets unrolled among the trees, the nodding trumpets shivering with each passing breeze. Primroses, too, and oxlips lined the path and golden celandines and everywhere among the dappled light, the startling greens of midsummer. Eventually the tree tunnel once carefully shaped and formed gave way to the true wild wood, breathing and alive around us.

We kept the horses to a walk, inviting the magic of the place to sense us, recognize what we brought, and decide if action might be required. The trees care little for our affairs. Their thoughts are not like ours; their consciousness reaches tendrils through all their lifetimes at once, and they have little to say to us that we can comprehend. Still, it is best not to bring an ill will among them. So far I had met acceptance and leafy indifference. For Random's part, the sharp planed features, cheek and brow, had visibly relaxed. When I glanced his way, he gave an easy smile, but I had a feeling he was in conversation with other voices and far away.

The path became narrower, rockier, and less manicured than it had been, until it meandered into three or four side ways, none much more than a deer track. My friend left me free to decide how to go, and so I did, well pleased at his confidence. The choice seemed so easy. The clue was the dash of spotted, bell-like blossoms that marched with us in a pink and purple haze. I thought they were the spears of faery armies, showing me the way. I failed to recognize the flowers until I had already leant over to graze them with ungloved fingers, and by then it was too late.

We rode on in the dead stillness of the inner wood as it grew darker and more tangled, more menacing. Even the horses barely disturbed the silence, and no birds sang.

Menacing? What nonsense, thought I with a small, unvoiced laugh. *Trust the gift, there is no danger here. Come in, come in, and come further in.*

On the other hand, if there were no danger, why were we here? For that matter, why *were* we here? And if there were nothing to fear, why was my heart racing?

"Wait," Random said suddenly. In that one syllable his voice, always so pleasant, dropped into the leaden air as flat and coarse as a raven's cry.

"What?" I snapped. We had hardly taken more than a few steps, I was sure, and I resented his intrusion.

"Listen."

"Don't be ridiculous, Random. What... Oh!"

At last I truly heard it: a lilting music, wild and strange. As if we had walked through a curtain into another room. Except I knew it had always been there, waiting for me long before I was aware of it. I will never be sure whether it was chimes or a bell, perhaps a flute, or even a singing voice merging with the wind. I only know that from that moment I rode in an enchanted wood where music filled the world with a gorgeous melancholy.

Random whispered, "Hold."

I reined in, or thought I did.

"Violet, stop!"

"I will. Let me be. What is the matter with you?"

Pale, impatient hands snatched the reins from my fingers. My eyes filled with tears but I had no idea why. All around me, pulsing lights of green and gold murmured and sang. Words, this time, in the loveliest voice imaginable

> *O fain would I be in the North Country,*
> *Where the lads and lasses are making of hay;*
> *There should I see what is pleasant to me,*
> *A mischief light on them that sent me away!*
> *Oh, the oak and the ash and the bonnie ivy tree,*
> *They flourish at home in my own country.*

I knew the song; knew and cherished it. Lady Laetitia had sung it to her children, and Random had played it for me. It had been mine once long ago, and was mine again. I would sing it to the swaying lights, dance with them too, if only—

"Miss Delacourt, report!"

I wish I could tell you that I snapped out of the terrible glamour at Random's barked command. I wish I had done so; the rest of the story would be less humiliating now. But Random dragged me out of the saddle by main force, practically throwing me to the ground. It may have been the hard jolt of hitting the ground that restored my senses, or the sharp sweet scent of leaves and bluebells crushed under my hands, or the three strange words of power shivering the air around me; but it was enough. The tactic did not immediately restore my balance, however, and for some time I stared owlishly into silver waistcoat buttons while he held my shoulders between his two hands.

When I was able to stand on my own, swaying but upright, he stepped back shaking his head. I sensed that rather than being cross, he was fighting the urge to laugh.

"My dear girl, I believe your next practicum will be the construction of a key to call you back from these little 'accidents', eh? In the mean time, perhaps you can resist gathering nosegays while ye may of every dangerous flower in the forest?"

A ring of low stones marked out the perimeter of the silent bluebell glade in which we stood. I sat down on the nearest one.

"Nosegays? I..."

I looked around, taking my observations. As he had told me before, curling ferns and brambles masked a low cave beneath an overhanging ledge of earth and massive rock. To one side a whitethorn tree, red with berries, overhung a lively spring, the source of the brook we had followed. Near it, a circle of cracked old white and brown tiles marked Wilgyth's well with its medieval cover laid back on rusted hinges. And here and there the spotted elf-cap blossoms rudely stripped from the foxgloves, rich with *phantastica*, lay crushed and scattered from my fall. They vanished at an idle flick of Random's hand and with them, a layer of sticky dust from my clothes and face —the deleriant material, I suppose. Such things have no affect on him, but as I may have mentioned, his magic is greater and more subtle than mine—if I can be said to have any at all. My mouth tasted oddly of vinegar.

"It took me by surprise," I said defensively.

"Again. We shall have to work on that."

"You heard the music, too!"

"The music was real, but it was meant for you. As it has been all along..."

Annoyed, I busied myself with straightening and patting at my clothes. Loose trousers, though cuffed at the ankle, plus a tight bodice with long full skirts proved not to be as practical as I'd imagined. Also, I seemed to be sitting on my pistol. A great bruise would be rising on my hip before long.

Finally, when I could face him, I said, "I believe we have reached the part of the drama where you say something clever, and then we dispatch a monster."

He considered this, then said, "Not quite yet. Tell me what you see."

I did so, noting also the compass points, the time of day, and the level I could perceive of paraphysical activity.

"And what do you take from all this?"

"A cave, a spring, a crystal well," I quoted, "Mark the place where spirits dwell. We're here."

"And we have already been attacked. So, where is the thing now, I wonder." Random walked to the open wellhead, where he peered down the shaft, considering.

"I cannot tell, *Magister*," I said stiffly. The scowl he turned upon me was more than I could bear. "No one knows where such things go when the sun drives them away. A spirit, a faery, if you like, is not an animal with a lair or a den."

"Except that it is here, else how could it have... Oak and ash, if I am not the lord high chamberlain of the kingdom of idiots!" His laughter had a bitter edge. "A lair, but not the well. By all means, let us learn from our mistakes. Violet!"

He hastened toward me giddy with delight, the black curls nearly standing on end.

"Violet! Get back!" Sparks gathered flickering about his fingertips. "Go on, yes, right to the edge of the clearing. Our friends are nearly here, and I must... timing... perfect!"

With no mind for my footing, I retreated through the bluebell carpet and into the trees. At the first of the sturdy oak trees I halted rather than fall among the knotted surface roots, turned, and fetched the revolver from my pocket. Falling on it had done no apparent harm, but I examined it all the same. I clicked the safety lever off and chambered a round. I could guess why they were special, these black rounds. A casing of silver will do for vampires, but for the Unseelie only cold iron will do.

"Ready!" I called, and looked up. "Random?"

Invisible? Vanished? He was nowhere to be seen. It is a skill I deeply envy.

"Here," he said. Wherever he was, the voice spoke in my ear. "Get down. Cover your eyes."

"Done."

As my knees hit the forest floor, a horrendous boom rocked the glade with the sound of a cannon's roar. Blasted earth and stone shattered and flew. And after it another, and a third. When I dared to look, I saw an image of Random possessed by his power sauntering toward the hillside and directing fire from his hands into the opening, sparks dripping from his fingers. As the rubble landed, I saw too that it contained scraps of jewelry, toys, ribbons; a child's doll, a silver christening cup. Mementos or trophies. Such tricks might not harm the boggart, and sunlight would annoy but do no harm. But to destroy its home, its new-claimed home, would enrage it, draw it to us, without question.

"Wee black dog come out to play," he was singing. "The moon doth shine as bright as day!"

He waited, listening, pushing a booted toe through the remains of a doll's house.

A mocking snarl sang back, "The oak and the ash and the bonnie ivy tree, they no more thrive in my own country. Oh, I'll have this and I'll have that, and make you the monkey in me old tin hat!"

Random Corwyn laughed and half turned unerringly to me. "Well, I see it's not to be a battle of wits. Tell me Lady Beckwith's maiden name again, please?"

I started to speak, but he put a finger to his lips, then to the side of his nose. He had remembered, or perhaps plucked it from my mind. The family name, the old attachment... There was a charm, but would it work?

"Boggart and braggart and Simson's Kow, Hob-o-the-hill, come now, come now!"

It worked. An evil face in a black cloud exploded out of the blasted hillside bellowing its fury. It rushed back and forth across the ring of the glade, roaring for revenge. What I could see of Random through the whirling dark, he appeared to stand fast, patient as a nurse waiting for a small child's tantrum to run down.

Revolver in hand, I watched too and waited. I've a temper of my own, you know, only mine has a bridle, and I drive it, it does not drive me. This cruel monster had killed so many for its revenge. It would never be satisfied. I only hoped its dispatch would come to me. And in that hope I raised my pretty pistol with its deadly loads, and prayed the boggart would take a form I could fire on.

Then it saw me, and I knew I had misjudged. "Random?" I called, too late. Faster than I could react and fire, the black mist reared up like a serpent of smoke, and arrowed swiftly to me, forcing itself through my open mouth and eyes into my body, into my mind. I was drowning, freezing, choking in the dark on the reek of mildew and cold hatred, but I did not fall.

The revolver remained gripped tight in my hand. When my eyes cleared, I could see out of them, but no more clearly than through frosted isinglass. Still living, I was trapped in my own body, screaming with barely a muffled sense of my voice. Overwhelming horror—no, I could not let it overwhelm me, though I had gone from observer to intimate, unwilling participant. And before me stood Random, motionless with a white-gold ball of energy contained somehow between his hands. He said nothing, only waited.

I felt my limbs move awkwardly, and not by my own will. When it looked down the length of the glade, I felt my mouth twist in a mockery of a smile. The boggart, well accustomed to manipulating small children and weary spirits, moved awkwardly in my limbs, and in my clothes. It stumbled on the uneven ground, tripped on my coat skirts and stepped through the wide trouser leg as it tried to right itself. At last it wrenched my body under sufficient control to raise the pistol to Random's chest.

"Miss Delacourt?" my friend queried under a flaring brow.

No!

"Aye! Yes, it's all right, dearest," I heard it say around the false smile, though the sound was muffled and muddy. "My will was the strongest. The poor wee thing is gone."

I despaired to hear my friend, my teacher's reply. I tried instead to somehow force my gun hand down, to point it anywhere but at Random. An iron bullet meant for the unseelie would kill a man just as dead. In fact, the boggart's hand—my hand—was trembling. The nearness of the iron, even though not in direct contact, had some effect at least, even if the force of my will had little, or none. I tried again, closing off all other senses.

No time! There was no time. Random would never be fooled by the creature's assurance, but whatever spells he launched risked my life along with the boggart's. As clever a magician as my friend was, I could see no solution except my death. If I could take the monster with me, I would accept it and gladly, but it was not my first choice. Perhaps I should have resigned myself to my fate and started praying, but what good would that do?

Then the small voice of my intuition whispered to me, "*Look up!*"

The wood around us had filled with horses and horsemen, too, in buff coats and bright steel helmets. Bridles jingled and someone coughed. The mortal world occluded, still those figures I saw clearly: soldiers of King Charles, eager for a fight. At their head, coolly waiting, rode a broad-shouldered man with a pointed auburn beard and mustache, long hair curling over a lace collar. A scarlet officer's sash wrapped his breastplate, and in the band of a soft, broad-brimmed hat a white plume fluttered in the breeze of some other day. Colonel Sir Robert Beckwith touched two fingers to the brim in salute.

Too late, his lady had cried to me. *He will come too late!*

Too late two and a half centuries ago, but now? And where was she? Where was Laetitia, the Lady Beckwith?

You may not credit all that transpired next, for it is longer in the telling than it took to occur, and to me it seemed to happen all at once. The facts are these.

I expected a cavalry charge, but they were only a feint; instead, a sudden blast of strength and beauty slammed into my chest and rocked me within and without. And as Laetitia's spirit entered, it sent warmth and strength coursing along every chilled nerve and icy pathway. Compounding our fury, both our voices sang out:

"Get out! Go! Vile thing, be gone!"

Its resistance drove me to my knees, but she lent her strength to my stubbornness and we pushed again. Freed and partnered, we spat it from me as a foul black smoke vomiting onto the grassy earth, burning as it came. We would have laughed but resolving out of that stinking mist, the black dog snarled and turned on us, bristling with fury, with blazing eyes and poisoned fangs. It charged. It sprang. My right hand came up when we asked it to, and together we squeezed the trigger as the creature left the ground. The little gun, seldom fired, kicked my hand and shoulder up, but no matter. We brought it into line and fired again. Then, bracing against the creature's fall, I turned my head to see the rest, waiting their turn: Sam the Smith, the cooper Digby, and Nellie Nesbit clutching her red vast cloak in her hands.

The bullets with their iron points, specially made, had not killed it, only trapped it in the last shape. Shape fixed, teeth snapping the air, the huge black dog would have fallen on top of me, but for Random. In the last instant he appeared and dragged me away just as it slammed to the ground where I had been. Before the boggart could regain its feet, Nellie had grabbed and held it in her strong dyer's arms to smother it in her woolen cloak, the scarlet color fixed in an iron pot. Enough iron, it appeared, to slow the creature even more.

"Now!" she cried.

Shorland the blacksmith stepped up and cast a length of iron chain around the thrashing bundle, and looped it round and round while Nellie moved aside. Then he threw the chain-trussed mass over his shoulder and carried it to the well. Beside it, Digby waited with his cooper's mall and some wedge-shaped iron pegs.

Sam looked back at Mr. Corwyn, who nodded.

"Do it."

"From ghoulies and ghasties," said Shorland as the big man cast the boggart bound into the well.

"And such long-legged beasties," Nellie said as it fell.

"And things that go bump in the night." Digby slammed down the old cover with its iron bands, and one by one drove the pegs in around the rim to seal it shut. No sound came from the well after the last blow fell.

"Good Lord deliver us," said Sir Robert Beckwith.

"Amen," Laetitia said.

She stood beside me now as she must have in her own time, the satin gown now crisp and new, her flaxen curls tied up with silk ribbons under a cap of fine lace.

I curtseyed as I had before. Dark eyes no longer hollow or bereaved, turned toward me. Not quite transparent, a radiance came from her like a star on the horizon. I tried to touch her arm in gratitude, but no substance met my hand. "My lady, you have saved my life."

"You and your folk have saved us all," she replied, her voice at last her own. "What was lost is found. He has come at last."

"My lady," Random said, appearing not quite from nowhere and looking extremely pleased with himself. He bowed, graceful as an elf, and offered his arm. "If you are ready, it is time."

I looked across the glade. All Sir Robert's faithful troops were already fading away to their reward, but he remained, and one youth carrying his banner. At his side upon a white palfrey, his lady sat like a picture in a storybook, and with them, three small fair-haired children on fat ponies of their own. Shy among the gentry, an entourage of childish spirits glittered near them among the bluebells.

Helen was not there but Random was, delivering a parting word to Sir Robert. And then, to crystalline music that was no song I have ever heard, he directed them onto a road I could not see, and they were gone.

Epilogue

We sent Nellie, Shorland, and Digby back to the village with
our thanks and the mounted footmen for an escort, while we rode
home in a companionable silence for which I was most grateful.
Mind and body abused and drained, I was in no condition to form
a question much less apprehend an answer. Random, too, looked
quite pale for his part in it.

At Corbisend, the Mayhews met us with grateful tears and a
very tired little girl. Young Helen had awakened with a sigh, they
said. Then she had sat up and mildly asked for her dinner.
Naturally they had fallen on her with hugs and kisses and thanks-
be-to-Gods. Mrs. Jenkins and the kitchen maids had brought piles
of buns and bowls of soup, and even a wedge of beefsteak pudding,
saying the girl couldn't have eaten anything wholesome in many a
day. She appears to remember little of her terrible ordeal, though
the truth of that remains to be seen.

The time of her restoration confirmed a conclusion I had
already drawn: the boggart, having chosen me, a willful living
woman, to "ride", had been forced to release them both. It could
not manage us all. A craven and a bully, human or uncanny,
cannot imagine what a woman of worth is capable of when free to
act.

My friend, their gentle landlord, gave Helen a gold sovereign
for her dowry, for which she thanked him with an endearingly
awkward curtsy. Then he sent them home in a carriage.

Next day, Mr. Random Corwyn sent workmen to collect every
bit of scrap iron in the district—Sam Shorland even contributed an
old anvil—as well as any that might be on the manor, and had them
cart it out to the blasted glade and bury the well under it. He
supposed it might be good to ask my father down for the fishing
soon, and perhaps the old fellow might be prevailed upon to
emulate that long ago Bishop Cuthbert, and pronounce an
anathema on the well site.

"My goodness," I said over a strong cup of tea. "Do they still do that?"

"I certainly hope so," said he.

The End

About the Author

Maggie Secara started out wanting to be an archaeologist. Then a reporter, then an international spy, a poet, an opera singer, a novelist, a historian. She ended up being a bit of each, earning a Masters in English and becoming involved with historical costume and improvisational theatre. When all those passions came together at once, she decided to be a novelist again, and so she did. Her short fiction has appeared in a variety of publications, including New Realm and Unsung Stories magazines. She is currently working on a Victorian ghost story.

Maggie lives in Los Angeles, California, with one adoring husband, two goofy cats, and half a million English words to toy with.

You can find Maggie in all these places:

Facebook   facebook.com/groups/maggiesworlds
Twitter   twitter.com/MaggiRos
Tumblr   maggie-secara.tumblr.com/
Pinterest   pinterest.com/maggiros/
Goodreads
goodreads.com/author/show/1632490.Maggie_Secara

If you enjoyed this book, please consider leaving a review to aid other readers in their choices.

www.ingramcontent.com/pod-product-compliance
Lightning Source LLC
Chambersburg PA
CBHW070649130626

46555CB00006B/2789